ÍN£

and the Treasure Box

Books by Jacqueline Harvey

Clementine Rose and the Surprise Visitor
Clementine Rose and the Pet Day Disaster
Clementine Rose and the Perfect Present
Clementine Rose and the Farm Fiasco
Clementine Rose and the Seaside Escape

Alice-Miranda at School
Alice-Miranda on Holiday
Alice-Miranda Takes the Lead
Alice-Miranda at Sea
Alice-Miranda in New York
Alice-Miranda Shows the Way
Alice-Miranda in Paris
Alice-Miranda Shines Bright
Alice-Miranda in Japan

CLEMENTINE ROSE
and the Treasure Box

Jacqueline Harvey

RANDOM HOUSE AUSTRALIA

Clementine Rose and the Treasure Box was conceived as part of a Creative Time Residential Fellowship provided by the May Gibbs Children's Literature Trust.

A Random House book
Published by Random House Australia Pty Ltd
Level 3, 100 Pacific Highway, North Sydney NSW 2060
www.randomhouse.com.au

First published by Random House Australia in 2014

Addresses for companies within the Random House Group can be found at www.randomhouse.com.au/offices

National Library of Australia
Cataloguing-in-Publication Entry

Author: Harvey, Jacqueline
Title: Clementine Rose and the treasure box/Jacqueline Harvey
ISBN: 978 1 74275 753 7 (pbk.)
Series: Harvey, Jacqueline. Clementine Rose; 6
Target audience: For primary school age
Subjects: Girls – Juvenile fiction
Dewey number: A823.4

Cover and internal illustrations by J.Yi
Cover design by Leanne Beattie
Internal design by Midland Typesetters
Typeset in ITC Century 12.5/19 by Midland Typesetters, Australia
Printed in Australia by Griffin Press, an accredited ISO AS/NZS 14001:2004 Environmental Management System printer

Random House Australia uses papers that are natural, renewable and recyclable products and made from wood grown in sustainable forests. The logging and manufacturing processes are expected to conform to the environmental regulations of the country of origin.

For Ian and Darcy, Flynn,
Eden and Baby Lawrence

NEW NEIGHBOURS

Clementine Rose chased the ball as it bumped and rolled across the front lawn. Lavender, her teacup pig, scurried along beside her, grunting and squealing. Clementine reached the ball first. She stopped it with her foot and then kicked it back towards Uncle Digby. Lavender spun around and ran after it.

'You two are going to be exhausted,' said Clementine's mother, Lady Clarissa Appleby. She was pulling weeds from the flowerbed beside the fence.

'I know,' Clementine puffed. 'Lavender will need a big rest this afternoon.'

Lady Clarissa grinned. 'I meant you and Uncle Digby, darling.'

'Oh,' said Clementine, giggling.

'I'm all right,' the old man protested with a flick of his hand.

'Well, I think I'm just about done here,' said Lady Clarissa. She dumped a giant clump of clover into the hessian sack beside her.

Digby rolled the ball gently towards Lavender, who pushed it along with her snout. 'You know, that pig's a natural with a soccer ball.'

'Maybe she can join our team,' said Clementine. 'You could too, Uncle Digby.'

Clementine couldn't wait to start soccer in a few weeks' time. She was going to be on a team with her friends Poppy and Sophie, and some boys too. Sophie's father, Pierre, had offered to be the coach and they would play in a local Saturday morning competition.

The old man shook his head. 'I don't think so, Clementine. I'm about sixty-five years too old to be playing in the Under 7s.' He walked over to Clarissa and reached for the sack. 'I'll take those weeds around to the bin.'

'Thank you,' said Clarissa. She removed her gloves and brushed some dirt from her skirt.

'Do you want to kick with me, Mummy?' Clementine asked.

'Maybe later, sweetheart. I think we should pop inside and have something to eat.'

The front door opened and Clementine's great-aunt walked out onto the steps. 'When's lunch, Clarissa? A person could starve to death in this house,' she harrumphed.

Lady Clarissa rolled her eyes at Clementine. 'We're coming now, Aunt Violet. I don't suppose you thought to make a start on some sandwiches?'

Aunt Violet winced. 'I wouldn't know where to begin.'

'It's not that hard,' Clementine chimed in. 'You just have to get the bread and butter and some things to put inside. I'll teach you.'

'Stop being so practical, Clementine. Some people were born to cook and others were born to eat. Clearly I fall into the latter category.'

Clementine wondered what that meant.

'Why don't you get your ball and bring Lavender inside, darling,' Lady Clarissa suggested.

Lavender had nudged the ball all the way across the lawn. Now it was stuck under some bushes by the low stone wall that separated Penberthy House from the road. Just as Clementine bent down to pick up the ball, a truck rumbled past. There were large letters written on the side and three men sitting in the front.

Lady Clarissa looked at the vehicle. A young fellow wearing a blue singlet grinned and waved at her. Clarissa raised her hand and waved back.

Clementine grabbed her soccer ball and raced over to her mother, who had joined Aunt Violet on the front porch.

'What did it say on the truck?' she asked.

'Griffin Brothers Removals,' Lady Clarissa informed her.

A silver station wagon turned into the road and followed the truck. A woman waved from the front passenger seat. Clarissa thought she saw some children in the back.

'They must be the new neighbours,' she said.

Clementine's eyes grew wide.

There was only one other dwelling past Penberthy House, a cottage at the very end of the lane.

'Godfathers, who'd want to live in that dump?' Aunt Violet said with a shudder.

Clementine shook her head. 'It's not a dump any more, Aunt Violet. It's lovely.'

'I can't imagine it. No one's lived there since I was a girl,' the old woman replied.

It was true that the place had been abandoned for years. Weeds and creepers had wrapped around the cottage's whitewashed walls, poking their way through cracks in the floorboards and into the house. The rafters were full of birds' nests and a family of rabbits had made itself at home in one of the kitchen cupboards. But that was before the builders had arrived.

Uncle Digby and Clementine had walked down to take a look at the progress the previous weekend. The house had been extended, re-roofed and repainted. Sitting in its pretty, tamed garden, it seemed as good as new.

Clementine looked up at her mother. 'Do you think there'll be any children?'

'I can't say for sure, but I thought I saw some in the back of the car,' Clarissa replied.

Clementine danced about on the spot. 'Can we go and visit them, Mummy? Please?'

'Not today, sweetheart,' said Clarissa. 'We need to give the family some time to get unpacked and settled. Maybe we can take them a cake tomorrow to welcome them to the village.'

Clementine felt as if she might burst. 'I'll help make it. It should be chocolate with sprinkles and chocolate icing.'

'Settle down, Clementine. They're only neighbours,' Aunt Violet said, rolling her eyes. 'The last family I remember living there had two of the most horrible brats I've ever known. They used to steal apples from the trees in our garden and their dog was always up here making a nuisance of itself. It would leave steaming messages all around the place.'

Clementine frowned. 'What do you mean, Aunt Violet?'

The old woman arched an eyebrow. 'Think about it, Clementine – have you ever seen a dog writing a note? What sort of messages do they leave?'

Clementine realised what her great-aunt was talking about and giggled. 'Oh. But we don't even know if this family has a dog.'

'Well, we can jolly well hope not,' Aunt Violet said with a grimace.

But Clementine would be very happy to have some children close by. Her two best friends from school lived in Highton Mill, and even then Poppy was on a farm a way out of the village. It would be lovely to have someone to play with after school.

'Come on, Clemmie, let's get those sandwiches,' called Lady Clarissa, as she walked through the front door.

Aunt Violet marched in behind her. 'A cup of tea would be nice too.'

Clementine lingered on the porch a little longer. She didn't care what Aunt Violet said. She couldn't wait to meet the neighbours.

CAKE MIX

Clementine licked the spatula, smearing cake batter around her mouth. She scraped the bowl one last time before Lady Clarissa scooped it up and popped it in the sink.

'But, Mummy, I wasn't finished,' Clementine protested.

'You were about to take the colour off that bowl, young lady,' her mother said with a grin. 'Besides, the cake will be ready soon and we still have to make the icing.'

'Can I help?' Clementine asked.

'Of course.'

The tantalising aroma of warm chocolate cake filled the kitchen.

Uncle Digby arrived back from Mrs Mogg's store. He placed a small pile of letters on the bench and then began to unpack the grocery bag.

'Hello Uncle Digby,' Clementine said.

'Hello. Something smells delicious,' said the old man. 'I think these are for you.' He handed Clementine a packet of chocolate sprinkles.

'Thank you. Do you want to come meet the neighbours this afternoon? Clementine asked.

'I'm afraid I can't. I have quite a bit to do. We have lots of guests arriving this weekend.'

The timer on the bench dinged and Clementine leapt down from her chair. 'It's ready!'

'Hold on, Clemmie,' said Clarissa, as she reached for a pair of oven mitts and opened the oven door. She pulled the shelf towards her and plunged a skewer into the middle of the cake. It came out clean.

'All done,' Clementine sang.

Lady Clarissa placed the tin on the cooling rack on the bench. 'We can mix the icing now. Then when we're finished, the cake should be just about cool enough to decorate.'

A little while later, Clementine finished shaking sprinkles onto the chocolate icing while her mother searched the pantry for a cake box.

'Are you coming to meet the neighbours, Aunt Violet?' Clementine asked the old woman, who had wandered into the kitchen in search of a cup of tea and was now reading the newspaper.

She shook her head. 'You can meet them first. And don't go inviting them for dinner or any such nonsense, Clarissa. We don't know anything about them. Probably not our sort of people at all.'

Clementine wondered who their sort of people were but decided not to ask. Aunt Violet was in a bit of a scratchy mood already.

Lady Clarissa told Clementine to run along and fetch a cardigan and give her hair a quick brush. The child scampered up the back stairs and returned a couple of minutes later.

'Can we take Lavender?' she asked, as she walked over to give the little pig a rub. Lavender and Pharaoh, Aunt Violet's sphynx cat, were in their usual position: snuggled together in Lavender's basket in front of the cooker.

'No, darling. We should see if the new family has any pets first. We wouldn't want to take Lavender and have her upset anyone, would we?' her mother replied.

Clementine nodded. That was probably the best idea.

A few minutes later the pair set off. It was about half a mile to the cottage. The pretty lane was bounded by a low stone wall on one side and open fields on the other. A trio of black-and-white cows grazed in the field. One looked up and mooed at Clementine, who mooed back.

'What if they're not home?' Clementine asked.

'Well, we can just leave the cake on the doorstep. At least we've had a nice walk.'

'But what if a sheep eats the cake?'

'A sheep? Which sheep?' her mother asked.

'Any sheep.' Clementine said. 'Sheep eat cake, you know. Just look at Ramon, the ram at Poppy's farm. He loves chocolate brownies.'

Her mother laughed. 'Clementine, sometimes you do say the strangest things.'

Clementine looked up at her mother and shrugged. 'It's true.'

They rounded the bend at the bottom of the road and, sure enough, the silver station wagon that had driven past the day before was parked in the driveway.

Clementine opened the front gate and ran down the path to the little porch. She looked at the door. There was no bell, only a brass lion's head knocker. She reached up and banged three times.

NEW FRIENDS

After a few moments, the door opened and a tall, thin man with a pointy brown beard and black-framed glasses looked at Clemmie. He had curly brown hair and wore checked pants and a dark-blue waistcoat over a white shirt with the sleeves rolled up.

'Hello,' he said, glancing from Clementine to her mother.

'Hello, I'm Clarissa Appleby and this is my daughter Clementine Rose. We live just up the road in –'

'Penberthy House,' the fellow finished. He had a huge grin on his face.

'Yes,' Clarissa said, smiling. 'Welcome to Penberthy Floss.'

'We're thrilled to be here,' the man said, nodding. 'And we're *thrilled* to meet you.'

Clementine pointed at the box in her mother's hands. 'We made a cake.'

'You must come in and have tea,' he said.

'We don't want to interrupt,' Lady Clarissa said. 'You must be terribly busy unpacking.'

Clementine frowned. 'But Mummy, you said that we couldn't come yesterday because they would be unpacking and that's why we had to wait until today.' She feared that her mother was going to turn around and head home. Clementine was dying to find out if there were any children in the house.

'No, we're glad to have a reason to stop.' He turned and called into the house, 'Ana, darling, put the kettle on. We have guests.'

Lady Clarissa and Clementine followed the man down the hallway. They skirted around packing boxes piled high, past a staircase, and through another door at the end of the passageway.

They stopped in a beautiful kitchen and family room. It was surrounded by windows with a view of the back garden.

'Ana,' the man said. A tall woman spun around from the sink with a kettle in her hand.

'Hello there,' she said, smiling.

Clementine thought she was one of the prettiest ladies she'd ever seen. Her blue eyes sparkled and her dark hair was pulled back into a sleek bun.

'Hello,' Lady Clarissa said.

'Oh my heavens, I haven't even told you my name.' The man hit the heel of his hand against his forehead. 'You must think me a real twit.'

'Of course not,' Lady Clarissa said. 'I can understand why you'd be distracted.'

'I'm Basil Hobbs and this is my wife Anastasia,' he said with an embarrassed grin.

'Please, everyone calls me Ana.' The woman switched on the kettle and lined up several mugs on the stone bench.

'It's lovely to meet you. I'm Clarissa Appleby and this is my daughter Clementine Rose,' Clarissa replied.

'We made you a cake,' Clementine said as her mother handed the box to Ana.

The woman lifted the lid. 'Oh, it looks delicious. The children are going to love this.'

Clementine's blue eyes widened. 'What children?'

'We have three, Clementine,' the woman replied.

An excited tingle ran down Clementine's spine.

'Our eldest, Araminta, is almost eleven, and the twins, Tilda and Teddy, are about to turn six.'

Clementine beamed. 'That's the same as me.'

'Actually, Basil, it's awfully quiet. Do you know where they are?' Ana asked.

'I think they've gone to see what Flash

thinks of the creek,' he replied. 'I'll give them a shout.'

'Who's Flash?' Clementine asked.

'He's the twins' tortoise,' Ana said. 'He's an adorable little creature. I must admit I never thought a tortoise would be affectionate or interesting but he's both.'

Basil opened a glass door that led out onto a deck. 'Mintie, Tilda, Teddy,' he called. 'Come out, come out, wherever you are. We have guests and they brought cake!'

'The house is beautiful,' said Clarissa as she looked around the room admiringly. 'And this kitchen is gorgeous. What a dream.'

'Thank you. We're very pleased with how it all came up, especially as we weren't here for the renovation.' Ana noticed the puzzled look on Clarissa's face. 'We've been away for months. Basil was making a documentary in France so we decided we'd take the chance to travel with the children. It won't be long until Araminta is off to boarding school.'

'How wonderful,' Clarissa said. 'The travel,

not that your daughter's going to boarding school.'

'Oh, she can't wait. We've got her a place at the new secondary school at Winchesterfield-Downsfordvale but she has another year in primary first. The children are all off to Ellery Prep this year.'

'The same as me,' Clementine said with a big smile.

Basil walked back across the deck. 'They're coming now.'

There was a flash of brunette hair and gangly limbs. Three children tumbled into the kitchen. They regained their composure and looked at the visitors.

'Hello,' the older girl said. 'I'm Mintie. It's short for Araminta.'

Clementine smiled at her. She had long chocolate-brown hair and blue eyes like her mother's. She was tall like her parents too.

'My friend Sophie has a cat called Mintie,' Clementine said.

'Good choice,' the girl said with a smile.

The twins were about the same height as Clemmie and had dark hair too. The girl's hair was tied up in two pigtails and the boy's was short and wavy but not curly like his father's. They both had brown eyes.

'I'm Tilda and he's Teddy,' the younger girl said, looking at her brother.

'But my real name's Edward,' the boy explained.

Clementine was wondering if the girl had a different name too. She must have read Clementine's mind.

'And my name really is Tilda and I don't like anything else.' She nodded decisively.

'You look the same,' Clementine said. 'Except for your hair.'

'I'm five minutes older,' Teddy said proudly. 'So she's the baby of the family.'

'Everyone knows the youngest is the cutest.' Tilda grinned.

Araminta wrinkled her nose. 'Says who?'

'Says your apparently very cute little sister,' Basil said, rolling his eyes playfully.

Clementine liked the family already. She looked at the patterned shell in Tilda's hands. It was about the size of a bread and butter plate.

'This is Flash. He's a bit shy sometimes,' said Tilda. Clementine could just see the curve of the tortoise's neck hidden inside his portable home. 'He's still getting used to things but he'll come out when he's ready.'

Tilda put Flash into a basket on the floor in the corner of the kitchen. 'That's not his real house. We've got to find it. We don't know where the men from the truck put it.'

'This is Clarissa Appleby and Clementine Rose,' Basil said. 'They're our neighbours.'

'Hello everyone,' Clarissa said. 'It's lovely to meet you all.'

'Do you live in that massive house near the corner?' Araminta asked.

Clementine nodded.

'Wow!' the twins said in unison. 'That's a mansion.'

'Are there ghosts?' Teddy asked.

'I don't think so,' Lady Clarissa replied.

Tilda's eyes widened. 'What about in the attic?'

Lady Clarissa shook her head. 'I'm afraid not.'

'Really?' The girl wrinkled her lip. 'I thought all old houses had ghosts.'

'Sorry to disappoint you,' Lady Clarissa said.

'I'm not disappointed.' Araminta shuddered. She wasn't keen on anything spooky. Tilda and Teddy knew it and loved trying to scare their big sister.

'Sometimes I think Granny and Grandpa are like ghosts,' Clementine said. 'I imagine that they fly down from their portraits and take tea in the sitting room. Grandpa loves poetry and Granny is always smiling.'

The twins looked at each other. 'Cool!' they said at the same time.

Araminta shook her head. 'Not cool.' But she couldn't help thinking that Clementine was just about the cutest girl she'd ever met.

Basil opened the cake box and lifted the chocolate confection onto a plate.

Tilda licked her lips when she saw it. 'Yum.'

The group settled around the table with cups of tea for the adults and lemonade for the children.

'How did you ever come to buy this place?' Lady Clarissa asked, before taking a sip of her tea.

'We've been looking for a home in the country for quite a while now. A friend told us he'd seen a little cottage for sale in Penberthy Floss,' said Basil. A sheepish look settled on the man's face. 'I have to admit I knew the village because of your house.'

'Our house?' Lady Clarissa asked in surprise.

'I make documentaries about grand homes, and Penberthy House has been on my list for ages, along with Highton Hall and Lord Tavistock's pile.'

Lady Clarissa laughed. 'I'm afraid our place is nothing like either of those mansions.'

'Perhaps not, but I'm sure that it has just as fascinating a history.'

'You're probably right about that,' said Lady Clarissa, nodding.

The adults continued chatting about the house while the children drank their lemonade and tucked into their cake.

'This is good!' Teddy said as crumbs sputtered from his mouth.

Clementine smiled.

'Do you have any pets?' Araminta asked. 'Daddy said that we're going to get a dog now that we live in the country.'

Clementine stiffened. She hoped it wasn't a dog that liked to leave messages. Aunt Violet would definitely have something to say about that.

'I have a teacup pig,' said Clementine. 'Her name is Lavender and she's at home with Pharaoh. He's Aunt Violet's cat.'

'A teacup pig!' Tilda and Teddy said at exactly the same time.

Araminta looked at the twins and shook her head. 'They always do that,' she explained to Clementine. 'You'll get used to it even though it can be a bit weird.'

The children fired a volley of questions at Clementine about where she went to school and what sort of things there were to do in the village and if she had a pony. They'd soon finished their afternoon tea and asked if they could take her on a tour of the house and garden.

'Yes, of course,' said Lady Clarissa. 'But we can't stay too long.'

'Aunt Violet will grumble if dinner is late,' Clementine said.

'Who's Aunt Violet?' Araminta asked.

'She's Grandpa's sister and she complains a *lot*,' Clementine explained.

'Clemmie, she's not that bad,' her mother said.

'Well, she was when she first came to stay and now she's never going to leave,' Clementine said. 'But I suppose we're used to her.'

The children scooted into the hallway and up the stairs, leaving Basil and Ana frowning and Lady Clarissa with a rueful smile on her face.

The children delighted in showing off every nook and cranny of the house, including a wonderful space in the attic with a whole lot of mirrors.

Clementine pointed to a long barre running along the mirrored wall. 'What's that for?'

'That's Mummy's, so she can practise,' Tilda said.

'Practise what?' Clementine asked.

'Ballet. She's going to start a ballet school in the village hall,' Araminta explained.

Clementine's eyes widened. 'I love ballet.'

'Maybe you can join Mummy's school. She's very good at it. I helped her choose the tutus that the girls will have to wear. They're red,' said Tilda.

'Do you learn?' she asked the children.

Araminta shook her head. 'I used to but I didn't really like it.'

'We do,' the twins said together.

Clementine's tummy fluttered. The twins shared a room and Araminta had her own with a bathroom between them. There was another room, which their father was planning to use as a study, and their parents' bedroom, which had a smart white ensuite with a beautiful big bath. Clementine thought Aunt Violet would have liked that a lot.

The foursome darted back downstairs and took Clementine into the garden. A lush lawn rolled down to a little creek. The children passed the raised garden beds, which were for a new vegetable patch.

'Uncle Felix said that he's going to build us a tree house up there.' Tilda pointed into the fork of an ancient oak. 'Daddy can't build anything but Uncle Felix can build everything. He fixed the house.'

'That would be amazing,' Clementine said. She loved the idea of having a tree house to play in.

A little while later, Basil called out that it was time for Clementine to go. The children were inspecting the newly constructed chicken coop, which was waiting for some residents. They raced back to the house.

'Mummy, there's a chicken house and their uncle is going to build a tree house and there's a play room in the attic, with a barre and mirrors for ballet,' Clementine said excitedly. 'Can they come and play tomorrow?' She looked at her mother, her blue eyes pleading.

'Of course, darling, if it's all right with Basil and Ana,' Clarissa replied.

'How about I walk them up after lunch?' Basil suggested.

'I can give you a tour of the house if you like?' Clarissa said.

Basil rubbed his pointy little beard and grinned. 'Oh, that would be splendid.'

'Why don't you all come for afternoon tea?' Clarissa said. 'Say, two o'clock.'

'You can meet Aunt Violet,' said Clementine, wrinkling her nose. 'And Uncle Digby. He's lovely.'

'Is he married to Aunt Violet?' Ana asked.

Clementine began to giggle. 'No way. Uncle Digby's much too smart for that.'

Lady Clarissa quickly explained who Uncle Digby was.

'Well, see you tomorrow,' Clarissa said as she and Clementine set off.

'See you tomorrow,' the children and their parents called back.

EMERGENCY!

That evening, Clementine talked non-stop about her new friends. Aunt Violet was out for the evening with Mrs Bottomley. It had come as a surprise to everyone that the two ladies had become friends after Clementine's class excursion to the farm. The pair had got lost after Mrs Bottomley was chased by a crazy goose called Eloise, and Aunt Violet had gone after them. Ever since, Aunt Violet and Mrs Bottomley had bonded each week over a game of bridge and a glass of brandy. It helped that they had a mutual dislike of children too.

Uncle Digby said it was just as well Aunt Violet was out, as she hadn't been very enthusiastic about the neighbours. She would probably be rather miffed about Clemmie's eagerness and her niece inviting them for afternoon tea.

'Mummy, my tummy feels fluttery,' said Clementine as Lady Clarissa tucked her into bed.

'Why do you think that is?'

'Maybe because . . . it's excited. The children are so lovely and Ana is beautiful, isn't she?' Clementine said as her mother stroked her hair. 'Can I have ballet lessons, Mummy? Please.'

'We'll see about that. And, yes, Ana is beautiful and the children are fun, and Basil's a bit of a character. I think we're very lucky to have the Hobbses as neighbours.' She leaned down and kissed Clemmie's cheek.

'I'm going to tidy up my room in the morning,' Clementine said.

Lady Clarissa looked around. Clementine's room was never particularly messy at all. 'Why do you need to do that?'

'So I can show the kids,' Clementine said. 'Then I can help you.'

'Ah,' said Lady Clarissa. Clementine clearly wanted ballet lessons a lot. 'You're very sweet. Love you.' Lady Clarissa stood up and walked over to the door and flicked off the light.

'Love you too, Mummy.' Clementine closed her eyes and within a few minutes she was fast asleep.

Hours later, just after the grandfather clock downstairs chimed three, Clementine woke up and realised she needed the toilet. The house was quiet except for the usual creaks and groans. Lady Clarissa said that the new roof would probably make all sorts of noises for a while. Clementine slipped out of bed and plodded across the hall to the bathroom, still half-asleep. As she washed her hands, she glanced through the sheer curtains and wondered about the red glow across the field. Clementine rubbed her eyes and pulled the curtain back.

'Mummy!' she yelled. 'Mummy! Come quickly.'

Lady Clarissa had been sound asleep. So had Uncle Digby and Aunt Violet. But within a minute the three of them bumped into each other on the landing.

'Goodness, Clementine, you'll wake the dead with that bellowing,' Aunt Violet grumbled.

Lady Clarissa pushed open the bathroom door. 'What's the matter, Clemmie?'

'Look!' She pointed out the window.

Lady Clarissa focused. Uncle Digby pulled his glasses out of his dressing-gown pocket.

'Good heavens,' he said. 'I'll call the brigade.' He raced out to the telephone on the small table near the top of the stairs.

Aunt Violet peered through the window, her eyes adjusting to the light. 'Oh, oh dear. I wonder what it is. Don't just stand there, Clarissa. We should see if there's anything we can do.'

'Aunt Violet, I don't think we'll be much help,' said Lady Clarissa.

'Godfathers, Clarissa, don't be so dull. It's the most exciting thing to happen around here for a jolly long time and I'm not about to miss it,' the old woman sniffed.

Clementine was dancing about. She wanted to see what was happening too.

'Well don't just stand there, Clementine. Get your dressing-gown,' Aunt Violet insisted.

The child rushed back across the hall to her bedroom. She pulled her dressing-gown from the end of her bed and dragged it over her arms, then stuffed her feet into her slippers.

Clementine hurried downstairs with her mother close behind her. Uncle Digby was in the entrance hall but Aunt Violet had disappeared.

'Has she gone to get a bucket?' Digby asked. 'I'll get the car keys.'

The wailing of sirens in the distance signalled that the fire truck was on its way from Highton Mill.

Aunt Violet thumped downstairs and elbowed Digby out of the way. 'I'll drive! We're not taking that clapped-out bomb of yours.'

Aunt Violet's shiny red car was parked out the front of the house. A minute later, everyone was strapped into their seats. The back wheels spun as Aunt Violet planted her foot on the accelerator. The car hurtled down the driveway, out onto the street and around the corner to the village.

'Look out!' Clementine called as the fire truck raced past. Aunt Violet swerved out of the way.

'Maniacs! We could have been killed,' Aunt Violet huffed.

'Aunt Violet. That's the fire brigade.' Clementine shook her head. 'You have to get out of their way.'

Aunt Violet followed the truck past Mrs Mogg's store and the church.

'What's on fire?' she asked, squinting to see.

'Oh no!' Lady Clarissa gasped.

'Well, what is it?' Aunt Violet demanded.

'It's the village hall,' Clarissa replied.

Aunt Violet pulled a face. 'Is that all?'

'Don't sound so disappointed, Miss Appleby,'

Digby said from the back seat. He'd just managed to right himself and remove the seatbelt from around his neck. 'What were you hoping for? Mrs Mogg's shop? The village inn, or some poor soul's home?'

'Don't be ridiculous, Pertwhistle!' Aunt Violet retorted. 'I just meant that I'm glad it's nothing important.'

'The village hall *is* important, Aunt Violet,' Clementine said from the back seat. 'That's where we have the flower show and the village concert and where Ana was going to start her ballet school.'

'Who's Ana?' Aunt Violet asked.

Clementine began to explain but was interrupted.

'Does the woman have any experience?' Aunt Violet asked. 'Ballet is an art form. If you're not trained properly you can do all sorts of damage.'

'Did you do ballet, Aunt Violet?'

'Yes, of course. I took lessons when I was at boarding school. You don't get to have my posture without years of training. We have to see whether this Ana woman knows what she's talking about. I'll insist on seeing her references.'

Clementine was no longer listening. They'd stopped behind the fire truck, and she was watching as the firemen rolled out their hoses and began pumping water onto the flames. Clarissa opened the passenger door. The sirens had woken the whole village and a small crowd was gathering on the footpath across the street.

Clementine hopped out too. She'd never seen so many people in pyjamas before. It was a bit like a sleepover, except everyone was awake. She was surprised to see Mrs Mogg's hair in rollers and Father Bob in his dressing-gown, which had trains on it.

'Please stand back, everyone,' the fire captain called. As he spoke the roof collapsed, sending a shower of sparks into the air.

'Oh!' the crowd gasped.

The villagers watched on, murmuring to one another, mesmerised by the inferno. After a

while the flames began to die down. The smoke was starting to clear and it was obvious there was not a lot left of the hall.

Another siren wailed and a few minutes later a police car pulled up in the middle of the road. Two men got out and talked to the fire captain, and then one of them turned around to address the crowd.

He consulted his notepad. 'Is Digby Pertwhistle here?'

The old man raised his hand and stepped forward. 'Yes, that's me.'

'You reported the fire, is that correct?' the policeman asked.

'Yes, that's right. But it was Clementine who spotted it first,' Digby said.

Clementine stepped forward next to Uncle Digby. 'I saw the flames when I went to the toilet. Mummy said that I shouldn't have such a big glass of milk before bedtime but I was thirsty.'

'Well, it's just as well you did, young lady,' the policeman said, 'or else this fire might have been much worse. It looks like they've saved the old stables and the shed at the back.'

'Clementine, thank goodness you saw it.' Mrs Mogg rushed forward and enveloped the child. 'I was sleeping like a brick. I didn't hear a thing until the siren was right outside the front door.'

'Yes, well spotted, Clemmie,' Father Bob said.

Clementine shrugged. 'I just went to the toilet.'

The flames were almost out, with some smouldering embers keeping the firemen busy. The other policeman was attaching blue-and-white tape to the fence to indicate that the grounds were off limits.

'Did anyone see anything?' the first policeman asked the group.

There was a collective shaking of heads.

'No, but come to think of it, after our quilting club meeting last night, the light switch sparked on me as I turned it off to leave,' Mrs Mogg said with a frown. 'Goodness, I hope I wasn't the cause.'

The policeman nodded. 'Mmm, sounds like it could have been an electrical fault.'

'You couldn't have known there was a problem, Margaret,' Lady Clarissa said to the woman. She turned to Clementine. 'I think we should be getting home.'

Clarissa and Clemmie bade goodnight to Mrs Mogg and Father Bob and the other residents. Aunt Violet had run back to the car as soon as she had seen how many people were about. She didn't know what she'd been thinking arriving in her dressing-gown.

'Where's Pertwhistle?' Aunt Violet demanded as Clemmie and Clarissa climbed into the car.

'Uncle Digby said that it would be safer to walk home,' Clementine said.

'Did he now? Well, he can remember that the next time he wants a lift anywhere,' Aunt Violet said through pursed lips.

'But he never goes anywhere in the car with you,' Clementine said. 'Except for tonight.'

46

'If he doesn't like my driving, then too bad.' Aunt Violet pulled away from the kerb and did a U-turn, narrowly missing the police car.

'Godfathers! Why on earth is that parked there?' she grumbled and sped off into the night.

AFTER THE FIRE

Clementine rolled over and yawned. She wondered if the fire last night had been a dream. Then she remembered Aunt Violet's driving. That had been more like a nightmare.

There was a knock at her door and Lady Clarissa entered. 'Hello sleepyhead. You must have been tired.'

'I couldn't remember for a minute if the fire was real, but it was, wasn't it?' Clementine asked.

'Yes, darling. It was real. And so was that terrifying ride in Aunt Violet's car.'

Clementine sat up. 'Can we go to the village and have a look at the hall?'

Her mother nodded. 'I've got to get the mail and a few bits and pieces from Mrs Mogg. Hop up and get dressed. We'll go once you've had breakfast.'

'Tilda and Teddy and Mintie are coming for afternoon tea today, aren't they?' Clementine said suddenly. With everything else that had happened she'd almost forgotten about her new friends. 'Oh no! If there's no village hall, where will Ana have her ballet lessons?' Clementine's face fell. She'd been hoping that Mrs Mogg would be able to make her a tutu.

'I don't know, sweetheart, but I'm sure she will work something out. The Hobbses are a bit protected down in that hollow at the end of the road so they might not know about the fire yet. I'll break the news gently to Ana this afternoon.'

Lavender waddled into the room, snuffling along the floorboards. She'd already been downstairs and back again, having hopped out of her basket at the end of Clemmie's bed earlier when the girl was still sound asleep.

'Good morning, Lavender.' Clementine slipped down from her bed and cuddled the little pig.

Lady Clarissa opened the wardrobe door. 'What would you like to wear today?'

Clementine thought for a moment. 'May I please have the yellow dress with the blue flowers?'

'Lovely.' Her mother pulled the dress from the hanger. 'And Mrs Mogg will be so pleased to see you wearing it.'

Clementine's love of fashion was well known in the village. It was something she shared with her great-aunt. But while Aunt Violet spent hours poring over fashion magazines, it was Mrs Mogg who created all manner of outfits for the child. She enjoyed nothing more than spoiling Clementine with new clothes.

Clementine dressed and went downstairs to the kitchen. Aunt Violet was at the table, nibbling on some toast and flicking through a magazine.

'Good morning, Aunt Violet,' Clementine said.

The woman glanced up. 'Morning. That's a pretty dress.'

Clementine smiled. 'Mrs Mogg made it.'

'I wish she'd think about making some clothes in my size,' the old woman said with a frown. 'I'd love something new. But I suppose I'll just have to make do for now.'

Lady Clarissa came down the back stairs just in time to hear her aunt's gripe.

'Aunt Violet, you must have the largest collection of clothes on the planet. I'm almost certain you could wear something different every day for the next ten years,' Clarissa tutted.

'That's quite beside the point, Clarissa. I'd like something *new*.'

'Well, unless you win the lottery, you're just going to have to put up with what you've got.'

Clarissa pulled a box of cereal from the shelves and shook some flakes into a bowl.

Aunt Violet pointed a manicured finger towards her magazine. 'Look. There's a competition here to win an entire new wardrobe.'

'Well then, you should enter it,' Clarissa said.

'No, Mummy, *you* should enter it,' said Clementine. 'You're much luckier than Aunt Violet. She lost all her money and her house. And didn't you lose some of your husbands, too?' Clementine asked, glancing up at the woman.

'Clementine Rose Appleby, the cheek of you!' Aunt Violet jerked her chair back and stood up. 'It's all yours, Clarissa.' She pushed the magazine to the end of the table. 'And you'd better win. That might go some way towards making up for that insolent daughter of yours.' Aunt Violet stalked out of the room.

Clementine looked at her mother. 'Did I say something wrong? It was the truth, wasn't it?'

'Yes, darling. But sometimes grown-ups don't like to be reminded of their mistakes, that's all.' Clarissa poured some milk into the bowl and set it down on the table.

Clementine dug her spoon into the crispy flakes and took a mouthful.

GUESTS

As the grandfather clock struck two, the doorbell rang. Clementine and Lavender skittered out of the kitchen to the front hall.

Clementine wrenched open the door and saw Basil, Ana and their three children standing on the porch.

'Hello, please come in,' Clementine said. She made a slight bow. Lavender gave a small grunt.

'Thank you, Clementine.' Basil doffed his stylish trilby hat.

Ana smiled but the children only had eyes for Lavender. They were just about bursting with excitement.

'Oh my goodness, she's adorable!' Araminta exclaimed. 'Can I hold her?'

Clementine nodded and bent down to pick up the little pig.

She passed Lavender to Araminta, and the pig immediately snuggled against the girl's chest. Tilda scratched the creature under the chin and Lavender repaid her with a nibble.

Teddy jigged about excitedly. 'She's so cute. Mummy, can we have one?'

Ana shook her head. 'I thought we'd settled on a dog and some chooks, and we've already got Flash.'

Lady Clarissa came through the hall and joined them. 'Hello everyone. Welcome to Penberthy House.'

Basil was busily gazing about the foyer. His eyes came to rest on the Appleby family portraits lining the stairs.

'That's Granny and Grandpa,' said Clementine. She pointed at a regal-looking couple halfway up the wall. 'And that's Aunt Violet when she was young and beautiful. She's not like that any more.'

'I heard that, Clementine,' a sharp voice echoed from the upstairs landing.

'Oops!' Clementine covered her mouth and everyone exchanged grins.

'And what is going on down there?' Aunt Violet's head appeared over the banister rail.

'Aunt Violet, I'd like you to meet our new neighbours,' Lady Clarissa said.

'You didn't tell me you'd invited anyone over, Clarissa.' The old woman walked downstairs. 'Especially since I told you not to,' she muttered to herself.

'Aunt Violet.' Lady Clarissa's voice was stern. 'This is Basil and Ana Hobbs and their children Araminta, Teddy and Tilda.'

'Yes, yes, lovely to meet you all,' Aunt Violet said wanly. The old woman reluctantly shook hands with Basil, then looked at Ana. She studied the woman's face and it was as if a light came on. 'Oh my heavens. You're Anastasia Barkov.'

Ana nodded. 'That's what I was called professionally.'

'Good heavens, Clarissa, why didn't you tell me that our new neighbour is the recently retired prima ballerina of the Royal Ballet?' Aunt Violet demanded.

'I'm afraid I didn't know,' Lady Clarissa apologised.

'Please, I wouldn't have expected you to,' said Ana. Her ears and cheeks turned a matching shade of pink.

'The woman's a national icon, Clarissa. I suppose that's the trouble when you spend your life out here in the country, devoid of all culture,' Aunt Violet said. 'I myself love the ballet. If only I were able to get up to the city more often. I have a subscription, you know.'

Clarissa eyeballed her aunt. That subscription had been cancelled along with various other luxuries her aunt could no longer afford.

'No wonder you were planning on starting a ballet school,' Clementine said. 'But now the hall's burnt down.'

'The hall?' Basil queried, clearly unaware of the drama. 'When did that happen?'

'Last night,' Clementine said. 'There were huge flames and lots of smoke and a fire truck and everyone in their pyjamas. Mummy and I went for a walk this morning, and there's a big pile of burnt wood where the hall was.' She nodded emphatically.

'Oh dear,' said Ana. 'That's terrible.'

'Clementine, I thought we'd planned to break the news gently,' her mother said.

Clementine's face fell.

Ana noticed at once. 'It doesn't matter, Clementine. It might just delay my plans a little. I'm sure they'll rebuild the hall.'

'The rate anything happens around here, my dear, I wouldn't count on starting that school any time soon,' Aunt Violet said. 'Perhaps you'd be better off to find another venue.'

'I've already investigated lots of other

places and the Penberthy Floss Village Hall seemed to be the only space available. We'll just have to postpone, I suppose.'

Clementine didn't like that idea at all. She was keen to start ballet lessons as soon as possible.

'Please, why don't you all come and have something to eat,' Lady Clarissa suggested.

Digby Pertwhistle had just popped the kettle onto the stove when Clarissa appeared in the kitchen with the guests.

She quickly introduced him and asked that everyone take a seat. Clementine had to show the children Pharaoh first, of course.

'He looks weird,' Teddy whispered.

Clementine nodded. 'I know. He's a sphynx. They've got no hair. But he's lovable and he's Lavender's best friend apart from me.'

'What are you whispering about, Clementine?' Aunt Violet demanded.

'Nothing.' Clementine shook her head. She knew from experience that it was better not to comment aloud on Pharaoh's appearance.

'Why don't you show the children where to wash their hands, and then come and sit down,' Lady Clarissa suggested.

She placed a large strawberry sponge cake in the middle of the table. There was another platter of brownies to follow and some home-made honey jumbles too.

'Goodness me, Clarissa, you must be the world's best baker,' Ana commented.

'I can't take credit for all this. Pierre Rousseau owns the patisserie in Highton Mill. He delivers cakes and bread for Mrs Mogg to sell in the shop so I snapped up the sponge this morning. The brownies and honey jumbles are mine but they're a cinch.'

Clementine and the children returned and quickly sat down, eyeing off the tasty treats.

'That's still impressive,' said Ana. 'I don't cook.'

'Not at all?' Clarissa said.

'No. Basil is in charge of the food at our place. With all my touring and strict diets and the like, I'm sad to say it's not something

I've ever mastered. Maybe you could give me some lessons?'

'Of course not,' Aunt Violet said briskly. 'A performer such as yourself, dear, has no mind slaving over a hot stove. I don't believe in it either.'

'But you're not a ballerina, Aunt Violet,' Clementine said. 'You just don't like cooking.'

Aunt Violet wrinkled her lip and looked away. 'And what about you, Basil? What's your line of work?'

'I'm a filmmaker,' the man replied.

'Oh, fascinating.' Aunt Violet was paying the new neighbours far more attention than anyone might have imagined. 'Feature films?'

'Documentaries,' Basil said.

'Oh. How . . . educational.' Aunt Violet barely disguised her disappointment.

'Actually, I was thinking I'd like to make a film about Penberthy House,' Basil said.

'A film about our house?' Clementine asked, her eyes widening.

Aunt Violet's did too. 'Really?' A smug smile began to form.

'Well, I'm sure it has a wonderful history and from the little I've seen so far, the house seems mostly original.'

'That's just a polite way of saying "tatty", Basil,' Lady Clarissa said, smiling.

'No, not at all. This place is a gem and I'd love to uncover everything about it. Of course, I need your permission, Clarissa. I'd want to feature the family too,' Basil explained.

Uncle Digby looked at Lady Clarissa, who in turn looked towards Aunt Violet, who was preening her hair and looking very satisfied with herself.

'I don't know, Basil. We've always been quite a private family,' Lady Clarissa said.

'How can you say that, Clarissa?' Aunt Violet snapped. 'You've opened our beautiful home so that all the riffraff under the sun can stay here.'

'It could be very good for business, Clarissa,' said Uncle Digby.

'Yes, Mummy, imagine if we were on the

television. Lots of people would want to come and see Lavender and Pharaoh,' Clementine enthused.

'Can I have some time to think about it, Basil?' Lady Clarissa asked.

'Yes, of course. I'm busy for the next couple of months anyway. We couldn't start shooting for a while yet.'

'Well, that will give you some time to get things in pristine order, won't it, Clarissa?' Aunt Violet looked at her niece. 'We'd want the house looking her best. And perhaps, Clementine, you can convince Mrs Mogg to make me something new to wear. I'd like to look my best too.'

'Are you in possession of a time machine, Miss Appleby?' Digby Pertwhistle gave the woman a wry smile.

'Very funny, Pertwhistle.'

The adults around the table did their best to smother smiles.

'Why does Aunt Violet need a time machine, Uncle Digby?' Clementine asked.

'I don't. Pertwhistle just wanted to borrow it so he could travel back and locate his hair,' the old woman quipped.

This time everyone laughed out loud. Even Uncle Digby.

THE ATTIC

Clementine and the children soon finished their afternoon tea and began fidgeting in their seats.

'Mummy, may we go up to my room?' Clementine asked. She was keen to show her new friends around the house, just as the children had shown her their home the day before.

Lady Clarissa nodded. 'Yes, of course, darling. I'm going to give Basil and Ana a tour in a little while.'

'I could do that,' Aunt Violet offered. 'Wouldn't you prefer to get on with the washing up?'

Clarissa glared at her aunt. 'No, Aunt Violet. The washing up can wait. But you're welcome to join us if you'd like.'

The old woman's mouth puckered.

Uncle Digby offered everyone some more tea.

'See you later,' Clementine said.

She darted away and the three Hobbs children followed her up the back stairs to the landing.

'What's up here?' Araminta asked.

'This is where the guests stay.' Clementine said. 'My room's on the next floor.'

She raced up the second flight of steps and along the corridor. Clemmie's room was at the front of the house, overlooking the garden. It was a large space with high ceilings and a pretty bedstead. She had a beautiful old rocking horse, which had been in the family longer than anyone could remember, and a doll's house that Aunt Violet said had been given to her as a child.

'What a lovely room,' Araminta said.

'This used to be Aunt Violet's bedroom when she was a little girl,' Clementine explained.

Teddy climbed up on the rocking horse and Araminta and Tilda explored the doll's house. After a few minutes, Clementine offered to show them the rest of the house.

The group followed Clementine back into the corridor, where she pointed out the bedrooms belonging to Uncle Digby, her mother and Aunt Violet.

Araminta looked towards a little door at the end of the hall. 'What's through there?' she asked.

'The stairs to the attic,' said Clementine.

'The attic?' Teddy's face lit up. 'What's up there?'

'Lots of stuff. Do you want to see it?'

'Yes, please,' the twins chorused.

Clementine opened the door and walked into a small corridor with a staircase. She flicked on the light.

Araminta hung back a bit. 'Is it dark?'

'No.' Clementine shook her head. 'But there's lots of junk.'

Teddy looked at Tilda and winked. 'I don't know. It looks pretty dark to me. And spooky. Don't you think, Mintie?'

Araminta frowned.

'Don't look so scared, Mintie. If there are any ghosts Teddy and I will protect you.' Tilda grabbed hold of her big sister's hand.

Araminta didn't want to believe in ghosts, but if they were ever going to see one, surely it would be in the attic of a grand old house like this. She hated that her little brother and sister were so much braver than she was.

Clemmie led the way. 'Wow!' she exclaimed. 'I can't see sunlight through the slates any more.'

But her visitors weren't remotely interested in the newly repaired roof.

They reached the top and Clementine flicked on another light switch.

The three visitors couldn't believe all of the

things that were jammed into the enormous space.

'Look at this.' Teddy ran over to a large dome, which contained a stuffed pheasant.

One side of the room was taken up by a row of old wardrobes.

'What's in those?' Araminta asked hesitantly.

'Dress-ups,' Clementine said. She guessed what was troubling the older girl. 'No ghosts.'

Clementine opened the closest wardrobe and pulled out a long ball gown. It was pink and had faded flowers around the neckline.

Araminta and the twins gasped as they realised that the whole wardrobe was crammed with clothes, and so was the next one and the one after that.

'That one there has hats,' Clementine said and scurried over to open it. She pulled out a black bonnet and popped it on her head.

'That's so cute,' Tilda giggled.

As well as the wardrobes, there was all manner of furniture, knick-knacks and household items.

'Look at this vacuum!' Teddy exclaimed. He picked up the handle. 'It looks like a spaceship.'

'What about this?' Tilda had pushed her way further into the room and located a gigantic globe of the world on a timber stand.

'There's a better one in the library,' Clementine said.

All of a sudden Araminta squealed.

'What's the matter?' Clementine called.

'Did you find a ghost?' her little brother teased.

Araminta hesitated. 'There's . . . there's a . . . creature . . .'

Clementine knew at once what the girl was looking at. 'No, that's just Theodore. He won't hurt you.'

'Are you sure?' Araminta squeaked. 'He looks real to me.'

Clementine closed the wardrobe door and hurried over to the girl. Tilda and Teddy followed her.

'Wow,' Teddy laughed.

'Hello Theo,' Clementine cooed. 'This is Mintie and the twins, Teddy and Tilda.' Before her was a stuffed warthog complete with tusks.

'Where did it come from?' Tilda asked, a look of horror on her face.

'Great Grandpa Appleby went on a safari to Africa a long time ago. Theo used to live in the library but Mummy said that he upset too many of the guests, so now he has to live up here.'

Araminta gulped. 'Are there any more creatures?'

'No.' Clementine shook her head. 'Mummy gave Boo to a museum. He was a lion.'

'I think it's awful how in the olden days people used to shoot wild animals just so they could have them stuffed and put in the lounge room,' said Araminta.

'That's what Mummy and Uncle Digby said too. Uncle Digby said that people weren't as smart about animals back then and they didn't realise they could become stink,' Clementine explained.

'Do you mean "extinct", Clementine?' Araminta asked with a smile.

'Oh.' Clementine giggled. 'That's what I meant.'

The children continued their explorations until they heard Lady Clarissa's voice.

'Clementine, are you up there?'

'Yes, Mummy,' Clemmie called back.

There was the sound of footsteps on the stairs and Lady Clarissa appeared at the end of the room.

'Goodness me, darling, I'm so pleased that you're showing off the most beautiful parts of the house.' Lady Clarissa shook her head. 'Have you taken the children to see the library and the sitting room?'

'Not yet,' Clementine said. 'We were going there next.'

Tilda's head popped up. She was wearing a striking pink hat with a long peacock feather sticking out of the top. Teddy had found himself an old triangular hat, which looked like it was from a navy uniform.

'It's fun up here,' the girl grinned.

'Yeah, it's way more exciting than our attic,' Teddy added.

'I just think it's an awful mess. One of these days we're going to have to sort it out,' Lady Clarissa replied with a smile. 'I'm glad you're having fun, but I have to interrupt it. We're all going to walk over to the village. Mrs Mogg called to say there's a meeting at the church to talk about the hall.'

Tilda and Teddy put their hats back into the wardrobe and the children made their way through the maze of bric-a-brac to Lady Clarissa.

'Is Aunt Violet coming, Mummy?' Clementine asked.

'Yes, I think she's having a lovely time with Ana and Basil,' Lady Clarissa replied.

Her aunt was being far more hospitable than usual. Clarissa had a sneaking suspicion that it had more to do with Ana being a famous ballerina than anything else.

'Can we take Lavender?'

'Yes, she needs a walk. Why don't you run along and get her ready. I'll take the children downstairs and show them the library and the sitting room and we'll meet you at the front door in a few minutes.'

Clementine nodded and scurried off.

The Hobbs children followed Lady Clarissa.

A few minutes later, the Hobbses and Applebys gathered out the front of Penberthy House.

'It's really a splendid house, Clarissa,' Basil enthused.

'Thank you, Basil. We love her, even though she's a bit worn around the edges,' Lady Clarissa smiled.

'So you'll think about the film then?' Basil's eyes twinkled.

Lady Clarissa nodded.

Aunt Violet tutted. 'Really, Clarissa, you should give Basil the go-ahead right away.'

'I'm a little surprised by your enthusiasm, Aunt Violet,' said Clarissa. 'When you realised that I'd opened the hotel you were less than impressed about sharing Penberthy House with anyone.'

'Well, that was different. Basil's team won't be nearly as invasive,' said Aunt Violet.

'I'm afraid we will be,' Basil said earnestly. 'The crew will have to stay here while we're filming, and I'll be doing lots of research to uncover everything I possibly can about the house and the family.'

'So you'll have to find out why Aunt Violet came to live with us,' Clementine said.

Aunt Violet's jaw dropped. 'That's quite enough, Clementine. My living here is of no interest to anyone.'

'I'm afraid you're wrong about that,' Basil said, rubbing his beard. 'People love a human interest story.'

'Yes, well, we'll need some more time to think about things won't we, Clarissa?' Aunt Violet glared at her niece, who could barely contain a smile. The old woman stalked off down the driveway. Basil frowned at Ana in puzzlement, wondering what Aunt Violet was hiding.

'Do you want to hold Lavender's lead?' Clementine asked Teddy.

'Yes, please,' the boy said.

'That pig is so cute,' said Araminta, as she and her younger sister walked along behind.

Lavender turned and gave a little grunt just as Araminta spoke.

'She always knows when someone is talking about her,' Clementine said with a smile.

VILLAGE MEETING

There were at least as many people in the village that afternoon as there had been the night before. But this time they weren't wearing dressing-gowns.

Father Bob was standing at the church gate welcoming everyone. Lady Clarissa introduced the Hobbses and then the group followed some of the other village residents inside. Mr and Mrs Mogg were sitting down the front and Joshua Tribble and his parents and older brother were on the other side of the church.

After a moment, Father Bob bustled down the aisle. 'Good afternoon, everyone,' he said. 'Thank you all for coming at such short notice. I've spoken to Commander Sprout of the Highton Mill fire brigade. Today the brigade conducted a thorough investigation and it seems that the fire was indeed caused by faulty electrical wiring.'

Margaret Mogg gasped.

'Please don't worry yourself, Margaret. It had nothing to do with you turning off the lights. The brigade believe the fire started long after that.'

A murmur went around the church. The villagers were glad to hear there had been no foul play involved and Mrs Mogg was relieved to know that she hadn't caused the fire.

'Now, as you've all seen, there's not much left of the old hall and what remains will have to be demolished. I'd like to thank you all for your support last night and I'd particularly like to thank Digby Pertwhistle and Clementine Appleby, who first noticed the fire.'

Uncle Digby was sitting beside Clemmie and gave her a nudge and a wink. Clementine's face felt as if it were burning a little bit.

Father Bob beamed at her and then looked around the church hall. 'Before I get to the most pressing business of the day, I would like to welcome our newest residents, Mr and Mrs Hobbs and their three children, to the village. We're always pleased to have new folk in town and I hope that you'll enjoy living here.'

Basil and Ana smiled. Clementine noticed some of the villagers craning their necks to take a look.

'Thank you, Father Bob,' Basil said. 'I'm sure that we are going to love Penberthy Floss.'

Father Bob nodded at him. 'Now, we need to work out how we are going to rebuild the hall. It seems that the insurance won't cover the full cost. Unless there is a builder willing to work for sandwiches and cake among you, I think we're going to have to put our thinking caps on and come up with some fundraising ideas.'

People began chatting at once.

'We could have a pet day,' Clementine called out. 'We had one at school to raise money for Queen Georgiana's Animals.'

Father Bob smiled at the child. 'Very good, Clementine. That's not a bad idea at all.'

'What about a fair?' said Mrs Mogg.

'Yes, we could have a fair but it might take a little while to organise,' Father Bob replied. 'Is there something we could do quickly?'

Basil leaned over and whispered in Lady Clarissa's ear. She turned to him and smiled. 'That's a great idea, Basil. If you think people would come?'

'Absolutely,' he said.

'What about we open Penberthy House and the garden and charge visitors a fee for a guided tour?' Lady Clarissa said.

There was a murmur of approval around the room. Aunt Violet glared at Lady Clarissa.

Mrs Tribble raised her hand.

'Yes?' Father Bob looked at the woman. He hoped her suggestion was sensible, given that she looked as if she might cry if it wasn't well received.

'What about a jumble sale on the lawn at Penberthy House at the same time?' she said.

'Oh, godfathers no,' Aunt Violet moaned. 'I don't think we want a whole lot of other people's junk masking the beauty of our home.'

Mrs Tribble's lip began to tremble.

'I don't know, Miss Appleby. I think that's rather a good idea. Surely we all have some bits and pieces at home that we'd like to clear out,' said Father Bob. He gave Mrs Tribble a wink.

'You're not getting rid of my toys,' Joshua whined. His father glared at him.

'What if we have a cake stall at the same time?' Mrs Mogg suggested. 'I'm sure Pierre Rousseau would be willing to lend a hand.'

'It could be like a mini fete,' Clyde Mogg said. 'Instead of a pet show, Clementine, perhaps people might pay to have their picture taken with your Lavender?'

Clementine's eyes lit up.

'We should take a vote,' said Father Bob.

Heads nodded all over the church.

'Who would like to support a fete hosted in the grounds of Penberthy House?'

Hands shot into the air.

Father Bob glanced around and noticed only one person without a raised hand – both of hers were firmly clasped in her lap.

'Miss Appleby, do you have a better idea?' the man asked.

Ana Hobbs turned to Lady Clarissa and whispered loudly, 'What wonderful community spirit. I'm so glad we moved here.'

Aunt Violet heard her and gulped.

'Well, Miss Appleby, is there something else you think we should do instead?' Father Bob asked.

Aunt Violet's hand crept upwards and she gave an ever-so-slight shake of her head.

'Splendid,' the man said. 'It's unanimous. Now, shall we set a date?'

It was quickly decided to hold the fete the weekend after next. Mrs Mogg was put in charge of the cake stall. Mrs Tribble would coordinate the jumble sale as long as donations could be taken straight to Penberthy House. Uncle Digby agreed to help her. They could store items in the old garden shed. Basil said that he'd be happy to contact the local newspapers.

Clementine was very excited about setting up a photo booth with Lavender. Araminta and the twins offered to help. Ana offered to paint signs and put them up around the village and some of the surrounding villages too.

'What about you, Aunt Violet?' Clementine turned and looked at her great-aunt. 'What are you going to do to help?'

The old woman thought for a moment. 'Supervise.'

'Aunt Violet, why don't you coordinate the tours of the house?' Lady Clarissa asked. 'You know the place better than anyone.'

Aunt Violet straightened her back. 'Yes, I suppose that's true. And then I could make sure that people don't go anywhere we don't want them.'

Lady Clarissa looked at Clementine and gave a sly smile. 'Of course,' she said.

PLANS

The villagers spilled out of the church into the sunshine. Clementine, Araminta and the twins took Lavender for a walk around the garden while the adults chatted.

'I'm so excited about the fete,' Araminta said. 'But I don't think we've got anything much for the jumble sale.'

Clementine's face lit up. 'We have heaps,' she said. 'In the attic.'

'Of course,' Tilda said. 'There's loads of stuff up there.'

'Me and Tilda can help you sort it out,' Teddy said.

'I can too,' Araminta added. She didn't want the little kids to think she was a complete scaredy-cat.

'Can you hold Lavender for a minute?' Clementine passed the little pig's lead to Tilda and ran over to where her mother, Uncle Digby and Mrs Mogg were busy discussing the best position for the cake stall.

'Mummy,' Clementine called, interrupting the threesome.

'Clementine,' her mother looked at her with a frown. 'What do you need to remember?'

Clementine bit her lip. 'Excuse me, Mummy.'

'That's better,' said Lady Clarissa.

'Mummy, can we have a clear-out for the jumble sale?' Clementine was bouncing about with excitement.

'Yes, of course. Do you have some toys you'd like to donate?'

Clementine thought for a moment. 'Maybe. But I meant in the attic.'

Lady Clarissa nodded. 'That's a wonderful idea, Clementine. I can't believe I didn't think of it.'

'We can finally get rid of some junk,' Uncle Digby chimed in. 'And then we'll have room to take some more junk up there.'

Clementine giggled. 'Can Mintie and the twins help me? We can sort it all out.'

'If it's all right with Basil and Ana, yes, absolutely. But there's a lot,' Clarissa said. 'It might take a while.'

'And not all of it's worthless, my dear,' said Uncle Digby. 'I think you'll find some treasures.'

Clarissa nodded. 'I could send the really valuable things off to auction and we can add that money to the fund for the hall too.'

Aunt Violet approached the group at that moment. 'What auction?' she asked.

Clarissa explained.

'And what exactly are you planning to do with the money?' Aunt Violet asked.

'Mummy said that we can donate it for the hall,' Clementine said.

'I don't think so,' Aunt Violet protested. 'You should be using it to fix that wretched bathroom I have to share.'

'We'll see about that,' Clarissa said firmly. She turned to her daughter. 'Clemmie, would you rather have a new bath or ballet lessons?'

Clementine's eyes lit up. 'That's easy, Mummy. I want to do ballet. In a red tutu.'

'Of course *you'd* want that,' Aunt Violet said with a sneer. 'I'd much rather have a bath without scratching my bottom.'

Digby Pertwhistle and Mrs Mogg smiled at one another.

'What are you smiling about, Pertwhistle? Your bath is fine. And you don't have to share it either,' Aunt Violet grumbled.

'Thank goodness for that, Miss Appleby. I can't imagine sharing a bath with you,' said Uncle Digby. He winked at Mrs Mogg.

'Digby Pertwhistle, you cheeky thing,' Mrs Mogg laughed. 'Oh well, I'd best get over to the shop.'

'Bye, Mrs Mogg,' Clementine called.

'Bye bye, dear,' said the old woman, waving.

Lady Clarissa looked at her watch. 'It's time for us to get home too. We've got guests arriving in an hour. Clementine, we won't be able to start any sorting until Sunday afternoon, when the weekend rush is over.'

'Heavens, I'd almost forgotten,' Uncle Digby said. 'But I think the house is in order.' He frowned at Clementine, raising his eyebrows. She had a habit of leaving things in the most inopportune places.

'It's okay, Uncle Digby. We played in my bedroom and the attic. I promise there are no surprises anywhere.'

Digby grinned at her.

Basil and Ana had met just about everyone in the village by now. Basil wandered over and Ana rounded up the children, who joined the group.

Tilda still had hold of Lavender's lead. The little pig was nibbling on a violet in the garden bed by the path.

'Mummy said that we can clear out some

of the things in the attic for the jumble sale,' Clementine informed her friends. 'Can you come on Sunday?'

The Hobbs children excitedly explained the plan to their parents, who thought it was a great idea. But they wouldn't be able to help until early the next week. They were off on Sunday for a couple of days in the city to celebrate their grandmother's birthday.

'When we finish unpacking, Basil can bring up some moving boxes. We've certainly got enough of them,' Ana offered.

'That would be wonderful,' said Lady Clarissa.

'I'll get a start on the signs tomorrow. The children can help me and perhaps Clementine would like to come down for the morning?' Ana said.

'Yes, please,' Clementine said.

The children skipped along in front of their parents, buzzing about the fete.

THINGS THAT GO BUMP . . .

Clementine was out collecting the mail with Uncle Digby when Basil Hobbs delivered a car load of packing boxes to Penberthy House the following week. Clementine and the children had painted the signs with Ana the day after the meeting and Basil had put them up all around the village and in Highton Mill too. But then the children had gone away and Penberthy House had been busy with more guests. Clementine couldn't wait to see Tilda and Teddy and Araminta again and to start sorting the attic.

Basil balanced several boxes and followed Lady Clarissa upstairs. When he saw the treasure trove in the attic, he was tempted to stay and help.

'Clarissa, if you don't mind me saying, please make sure that you check the children's decisions on what can go into the jumble sale,' the man said as he spied a stunning Tiffany lamp on top of a mahogany side table.

'Yes, I certainly will, Basil. I thought that they could be in charge of the more ordinary household items.' Lady Clarissa picked up a cracked pie plate. 'Like this. Uncle Digby and I will look after everything else.'

Basil wandered to the other end of the room. 'Oh my heavens, where did you get him?'

'I presume you've found Theo.' Lady Clarissa edged through the furniture to join the man. 'He's very handsome, don't you think?'

'He'd scare the socks off anyone,' Basil grinned.

'That's why he's up here. He was in the library until one of our guests took a walk in the middle of the night. The poor woman screamed so loudly I thought there must have been an intruder. When I found her she was as white as a sheet and frozen to the spot, demanding that I call the police and have the animal shot. I didn't have the heart to tell her that my grandfather had already done that about eighty years earlier. The next day Uncle Digby and I heaved and hefted Theo up here. You know, he's awful but I just can't bear to part with him. He's been in the family for such a long time.'

'He'd have to be sent to auction anyway, Clarissa. There must be collectors who delight in that sort of thing. It's not my cup of tea but someone would love him,' Basil said as he cast his eyes over the rest of the bric-a-brac. 'I should get going. The children couldn't fit in the car with me and all the boxes but they'll be up soon.'

Lady Clarissa had just farewelled Basil and was on her way to the kitchen when she heard the back door slam.

'Are they here yet?' Clementine called as she almost bumped into her mother. She'd been bursting to see the Hobbs children again for days.

'Hello darling, did you have a good walk?'

Clementine nodded.

The doorbell rang.

'They're here!' Clementine raced into the hall and skidded along the polished timber floorboards in her socks. She wrenched open the front door.

'Hello,' Clementine said.

'Hi,' the twins chorused.

'Hello,' Araminta said.

Lady Clarissa walked up behind Clementine. 'Good morning. Your father dropped off the boxes a few minutes ago. Come in.'

'How was your grandmother's birthday celebration?' Lady Clarissa asked.

'It was fun. Granny had a huge cake and it had about a hundred candles on it,' Tilda said.

'It was only eighty, Tilda,' said Araminta, shaking her head.

'That's even more than Aunt Violet,' Clementine said. She couldn't imagine that many people in the world were older than her. 'Can we go upstairs, Mummy?'

Lady Clarissa nodded. 'I think I might help for a little while. There's a lot to get through. And then I have to make some phone calls and do some paperwork.'

Clementine nodded. 'We can do it, Mummy. I promise.'

Lady Clarissa smiled at the eager foursome. 'Come on, then. Let's go and do battle, shall we?'

The children followed Lady Clarissa up to the attic. She had already pulled back the shutters to let in as much light as possible.

'Now, I thought you could find anything that was household related. Like the vacuum, and the pots and pans down the back. There's a huge number of old kitchen utensils, too. Why don't you stack them into boxes and then I can have a look afterwards. Uncle Digby and I will take care of all the decorative things and the furniture and maybe Aunt Violet can help with the clothes.'

'Oh no, Mummy, please don't sell the dress-ups,' Clementine begged.

'You know, Mummy said that when the ballet school is up and running, she'd have a concert at the end of every year. Some of the clothes would be perfect for that,' Araminta said.

Clementine nodded. 'That's a great idea.'

Her mother relented with a smile. 'Okay, Clementine, the clothes can stay. Now, does everyone know what they're looking for?'

'Yes,' the children chorused. Clementine, Tilda and Teddy headed straight to the far end of the attic.

'I think there's an old mixer down here,' Clementine said.

Araminta got started on a huge old dresser full of cutlery and utensils.

Lady Clarissa spent about fifteen minutes watching them. When she was satisfied that they weren't about to put anything especially valuable in the boxes, she headed downstairs.

'Hey, look at this,' Araminta called. Clementine and the twins made their way to the other side of the attic.

'What is it?' Tilda asked.

Clementine looked at the bowl. 'I've seen one of those before,' she said. She suddenly remembered. 'Oh! That's an old-fashioned toilet.'

'Yuck,' said Araminta. She peered inside. 'At least it's clean.'

Teddy looked at it too. 'I wonder how many of your relatives have used that.'

Clementine shrugged. The children continued their sorting and packing and were surprised that they already had six boxes of household items for the stall.

'Does anyone feel like a drink?' Clementine asked.

The children nodded. Araminta wiped some beads of perspiration from her brow. 'I thought you were never going to ask.'

'Let's get some morning tea and come back later,' Clementine said.

Just as they were about to leave, there was a loud thud.

'What was that?' Teddy said.

The children looked to see if anything had fallen over.

'Probably just something in one of the cupboards falling down,' Clementine said confidently. She walked over to the first wardrobe and opened the doors, but everything was still in place. She wandered along and opened each one but couldn't see anything unusual.

There was another thud, this time louder than the first.

Araminta jumped. 'Can we go?' she said, her knees trembling.

'It's all right. I've been up here lots of times,' Clementine said. 'It's probably a mouse.'

Teddy had wandered off into the far corner of the room and discovered a narrow door.

'Clementine, where does this go?' the boy called.

Clementine scampered over with Tilda and Araminta behind her. She couldn't remember seeing the door before. Maybe her mother had moved something out of the way earlier.

'Open it,' she said.

Teddy turned the handle, wondering what he'd find.

It was certainly not what he was expecting.

'Ahhhh!' the twins and Araminta screamed in unison. 'It's a skeleton!'

The three Hobbs children raced off towards the stairs. Clementine giggled. So much for the twins wanting to find a ghost. But Clementine wasn't frightened. She peeked in.

'Hello, who are you?' she said. She was about to leave when she heard a scraping noise. It was loud and didn't sound like any of the mice she'd come across before. She jumped and ran down the attic stairs, along the hall and down

the back stairs to the kitchen. She found her friends all talking at once, telling Lady Clarissa about the thuds and the skeleton in the other room.

'Mummy, I told the children there was nothing up there but when I looked at the skeleton, I heard a scraping noise and I didn't know what it was either. Where did the skeleton come from? Is it someone in the family?' Clementine fired the questions at her mother.

Lady Clarissa directed the children to sit down. She pulled a large pitcher of homemade lemonade out of the fridge and set it down on the table.

'The skeleton's nothing to worry about. I'd forgotten about him actually,' she said. 'He first belonged to your great-grandfather, Clementine. He was a doctor and that skeleton was affectionately known as Claude. We inherited him. Your grandmother used to love playing tricks on your grandfather with him. She'd put him in all sorts of odd places around the house when I was a girl and then wait for your grandpa to bellow. She and I loved it. Uncle Digby used to get in on the act too, I think,' Lady Clarissa explained.

The old man walked into the room balancing a tea tray. He'd just served morning tea to the guests who'd arrived the previous evening.

'What did I do?' he asked, setting the tray on the bench near the sink.

'The children discovered Claude upstairs in the attic,' Lady Clarissa explained. 'Do you remember that time Mummy and I took Claude and set him up in Daddy's office chair in the library? The poor man almost had a heart attack when he spun the chair around and went to sit down.'

'Oh yes, that was funny. But I think the best one was when we put him in the back of your father's car with a hat and a coat. Your father was halfway to Highton Mill before he realised who his passenger was,' Uncle Digby said with a giggle. 'Although that was very silly of us.

In hindsight, the poor man could have had a nasty accident.'

The children listened to the stories and felt much better about the skeleton.

'But that still doesn't explain the thuds and the scraping sound,' Araminta said, frowning.

'It could have been anything,' said Uncle Digby. 'And I might just set a few rat traps in case the builders let some creatures in while the roof was being done.'

'Was it Lavender?' Lady Clarissa asked. 'Or Pharaoh?' Both animals were missing from their usual spot in Lavender's basket.

Clementine shook her head. 'I didn't see either of them up there and usually Pharaoh meows so loudly to let you know he's around.'

'I wonder if it really could be a ghost,' Tilda said. 'Daddy says that all old houses have ghosts.'

Araminta flinched. 'I don't want to go up there again.'

'I've lived here all my life and I've never seen any ghosts. Why don't you go and play in the garden for a little while and get some fresh air,' Lady Clarissa suggested. 'You can do some more sorting later, if you like.'

While the attic was a treasure trove, outside the sun was shining and the skeleton had put the visitors off going back upstairs for now.

'Do you want to play hide-and-seek?' Clementine asked.

'Okay,' Tilda and Teddy said at the same time.

Araminta nodded.

Lady Clarissa set a plate of chocolate-chip biscuits on the table.

'Why don't you take these into the garden,' she said. 'I'll see if I can find Lavender and Pharaoh and shoo them out.'

Before she could move, a squeal came from the sitting room.

'Oh, oh, what on earth?' a woman called loudly. 'Good gracious, there's a monster in here.'

'Oops! I think our guests have just met Pharaoh.' Lady Clarissa dashed off.

Clementine giggled and the others did too.

GONE IN A FLASH

Clementine and her friends played hide-and-seek, followed by chasings, stuck in the mud and a rowdy game of soccer. Teddy and Tilda said that they were eager to join Clementine's Saturday team if there was room for a couple more players. Clementine thought that was a great idea.

Lady Clarissa had rescued Pharaoh from the startled guests and quickly located Lavender. The pair were sent outside with the children. Lavender couldn't decide which side she was on, chasing the ball in both directions. Pharaoh wasn't remotely interested. He jumped up on one of the outdoor chairs and promptly fell asleep.

Uncle Digby made the children some sandwiches and they ate lunch outside. Ana arrived sooon afterwards.

She walked onto the back steps with Lady Clarissa. 'Hello everyone, how's the attic sorting?'

'We got six boxes done, but then Mintie got scared,' Teddy said.

Araminta glared at her brother. 'It wasn't just me. You and Tilda ran away too.'

'I hope you've been helpful,' Ana said. 'Anyway, I'm sorry, kids, but we have to get going. I almost forgot that you're all having haircuts this afternoon in Highton Mill.'

Clementine and her mother watched and waved as the Hobbses' car drove out the driveway.

'Now, why don't you and I do some more sorting,' Lady Clarissa suggested. 'Uncle Digby said he has a bit of time now too. The guests have gone for a long drive and won't be back until dinnertime.'

'Okay, Mummy,' Clementine said, and the two walked upstairs. She wasn't scared about being up there with her mother and Uncle Digby.

Digby Pertwhistle had already pulled out an interesting array of lamps, ornaments and statues. He was waiting for Clarissa to help move some of the larger pieces.

'Goodness, what have you found, Uncle Digby?' Clarissa asked as she surveyed the items.

'Oh, this and that. But there's lots more.'

'What do you want me to do, Mummy?' Clementine asked.

'Hmm, why don't you see what's in the dresser in the back corner.'

Clementine scurried off, saying hello to Theodore on her way. She opened the dresser drawers and found a whole set of knives and forks and spoons. Clementine dumped them into a box that one of the twins had moved to the far end of the attic.

She opened the dresser doors and found three different-sized wooden boxes.

'Mummy, what are these?' she called.

Lady Clarissa made her way over.

'Oh, they're music boxes. The smallest one was mine when I was little. I kept all my precious things inside. I'd forgotten about it. I don't know where the others came from.'

Lady Clarissa pulled out the box that belonged to her. She opened the lid and a beautiful ballerina sprang up on a platform.

Clementine gasped. 'Does she dance?'

Her mother turned the box around and found a little winder. She gave it a crank and put the box on the dresser. Music began to play and the tiny dancer started to twirl.

'Mummy, she's lovely,' Clementine said. 'Can I keep her?'

Lady Clarissa nodded. She reached in and pulled out a slightly larger box. This time when

she lifted the lid, the ballerina was broken and the lining torn.

'I think this one can go out,' she said, and placed it in the box with the cutlery.

The last box was almost twice the size of the others. Inside, the ballerina was tatty and no longer twirled. Clarissa was about to put it in with the goods for the fete when the telephone rang.

'I'll get it, Clarissa,' Digby called from the other end of the room.

'No, don't you run. I'll go.' Clarissa put the music box on the floor and dashed as quickly as she could to the telephone in the hall on the third floor. She didn't like the old man rushing. A health scare earlier in the year had landed him in hospital and given them all a nasty fright.

Clementine stared at her twirling ballerina. When the music stopped she wound the spring again and again, listening to the same tune chiming over and over.

Her mother returned and began to help Uncle Digby move several side tables.

'Clemmie, why don't you take that and show Aunt Violet,' she suggested.

'Okay, Mummy.'

Uncle Digby grinned. 'Thank you, Clarissa,' he whispered. 'I don't think I want to hear that tune ever again.'

Clementine didn't see the little creature crawl its way into the largest box, which her mother had left sitting open on the floor. And over the din of the chimes, she didn't hear the scraping noise that had startled her earlier. Clementine picked up her new treasure and spun around, almost tripping over the box on the floor. She kicked the lid with her foot and it snapped shut.

Clementine put her precious music box on the dresser and picked up the other one from the floor. 'You're supposed to be in there.' She deposited it into the cardboard box for the fete.

'See you later,' she said to her mother and Uncle Digby as she sped downstairs to find Aunt Violet.

'You know your aunt won't thank you for sending Clementine in her direction,' Uncle Digby smiled.

Lady Clarissa grinned. 'No, I'm sure to hear about it later, although I think we might have sent Clemmie on a wild goose chase. I've just remembered that Aunt Violet's gone to visit Mrs Bottomley. Let's just get this done and we can go and have a cup of tea.'

FETE DAY

Clementine woke up just as the clock in the hall struck seven. She rushed to the window. The afternoon before, some men had put up a stripy blue marquee on the front lawn for Mrs Mogg's cafe. In the dim morning light, Clementine could see Father Bob and Mr Mogg moving trestle tables with Mrs Tribble directing them.

Clementine ran to the wardrobe and pulled out her favourite red dress and matching shoes. She quickly got dressed and brushed her hair, pinning it back with a red bow.

Lavender was making snuffly grunts in her basket at the end of the bed. Clementine decided to let the little pig sleep. She needed her to look her best for the photographs.

Clementine, Araminta and the twins had spent the previous afternoon finding the perfect backdrop for Lavender's photo booth. They had tossed up between the rose garden out the front and the fountain around the back of the house. It was Lady Clarissa who decided that it would be better for business if they stayed close to the stalls in the front garden. Basil was going to be the photographer for the day.

Clementine was worried about her new friends. A few days before, Flash had gone missing from the Hobbses' house and, although the children had searched high and low, there was no sign of him. Clementine remembered how worried she'd been when Lavender had escaped at the seaside. Tilda was especially upset.

'I'll come back and get you ready after breakfast,' Clementine whispered to Lavender, and then raced into the hallway.

Aunt Violet was walking towards her, carrying a thick plait of red rope and a box of pins.

'You look nice, Aunt Violet.' Clementine admired the woman's smart navy pants-suit and spotty silk blouse. 'What are you doing?'

'I'm roping off all the areas of the house where we don't want people to go.'

Clementine looked down the hallway. The rope was across the top of the main stairs. She took a few steps further and noticed that there was another rope blocking off the floor below. She wondered if the people were going to get any further than the front hall.

'Now run along, Clementine, and don't touch any of my ropes,' Aunt Violet directed.

The kitchen was buzzing. People were coming in and out of the back door, bringing all sorts of delicious treats, and Mrs Tribble was now directing her husband and Mr Mogg as they moved the last of the boxes from the Penberthy House attic.

Mrs Mogg turned from where she was arranging chocolate brownies on a plate. 'Good morning, Clementine. Don't you look lovely.'

'I can't wait for the fete.' Clementine shivered with excitement.

She poured herself some cereal, and Mrs Mogg offered to help with the milk. Usually Clementine liked to do things herself but this morning she didn't want to spill anything on the table or her dress.

Aunt Violet stormed into the kitchen. Her face was red and Clementine could almost see the steam coming out of her ears. 'Who took the rope from the bottom of the staircase?'

Lady Clarissa came down the back stairs at that moment. 'I did, Aunt Violet. You've got hours until the tours begin and I needed to bring some more things downstairs for the jumble sale.'

'What do you call those?' Aunt Violet pointed at the back stairs.

'Aunt Violet, I was trying to take the shortest route to the front garden. Those boxes are heavy, you know.'

'Don't get snippy with me, Clarissa. I've got a lot to do. If you want these tours to work, I simply can't have people traipsing all through the house. There . . . there are rules!' She turned on her heel and strode from the room.

'Her rules,' Uncle Digby muttered.

Clementine finished her breakfast and raced upstairs to get Lavender ready. She was going to wear her best sparkly red collar with the matching lead.

By nine o'clock the stalls were set up, Mrs Mogg's cafe was ready and Aunt Violet had finished roping off the house. As far as Clementine could tell, guests would be allowed in the sitting room, dining room, conservatory and library. Everywhere else was off limits.

Clementine recognised lots of things on Mrs Tribble's bric-a-brac tables but there was loads more that other people in the village had donated too.

Basil and Ana arrived with the children in tow. Clementine and Lavender raced out to greet them.

'Hello,' Clementine said. 'Lavender's all ready for the photos.'

Basil grinned. 'And might I say she looks especially gorgeous today.'

'I'd better get going and help Mrs Tribble,' Ana said.

'Have you found Flash?' Clementine asked.

Tilda shook her head. 'I don't think he's ever coming back.'

'He might have walked home to our old house,' Araminta said. 'I've heard stories of cats and dogs who do that.'

'Then he'll be there in about ten years' time,' Teddy said. 'He's not exactly fast, is he?'

'Stop saying that,' Tilda said sulkily. 'You don't care about him.'

'Yes, I do,' Teddy said. 'He's my tortoise too.'

'But you don't look after him as much as I do.' Tilda's eyes glistened.

'Sorry, Tilda.' Teddy put his arm around his twin sister. 'I'm sure he'll come home.' Teddy wasn't sure at all, but at least if Flash had escaped outside he had a nice place to live by the creek with plenty of things to eat.

'Why don't you go and get your booth ready?' Basil suggested. 'Have you got the money tin and some change sorted?'

Soon the crowds began to pour into the garden. Aunt Violet insisted that she wasn't taking any tours until ten o'clock but by nine-thirty there was a line of people waiting to go in. Mrs Bottomley had come along to help her, so after quite a bit of discussion Aunt Violet decided to open early. She had thought about upping the price for the inconvenience but Mrs Bottomley talked her out of it.

Clementine and her friends were doing great business in their photo booth.

Lavender was behaving perfectly, sitting beside the eager children and adults while Basil snapped away. Tilda and Teddy were taking people's names and telling them what time they could come and collect their pictures, while Araminta was in charge of the money. Clementine made sure that Lavender was feeling all right and not too tired.

By early afternoon the children were starving and Basil said that they should shut up shop for a while and take a break. 'Besides,' he said, 'Lavender has been smiling so much her face must be sore.'

'Lavender can't smile,' Clementine said with a giggle.

Basil winked. 'I don't know, Clementine. I think she can.'

There was a jumping castle that the children had their eyes on and a lucky dip stall that they wanted to visit.

Aunt Violet decided that she and Mrs Bottomley were due for a break too.

Mrs Bottomley was keen to have a quick look at the stalls before the best things were gone.

The crowds had thinned out a bit since the morning rush but Lady Clarissa couldn't believe how much they had already raised.

'What a wonderful day, Clarissa,' Father Bob said as he walked into the kitchen to hand over another tin of money from his flower stall. 'I think we'll have that new hall built sooner than we thought.'

Clarissa smiled. She certainly hoped so.

TREASURE

Clementine and her friends wandered into Mrs Mogg's cafe.

'Hello there, my lovelies. What can I get you?' the woman called.

'May I please have a vanilla milkshake and a chocolate brownie?' Clementine asked. 'And a bowl of water for Lavender, please.'

The other children all ordered chocolate milkshakes and a variety of cupcakes.

Clementine reached into her pocket and

handed over a crisp note. 'It's my pocket money,' she said proudly.

Araminta paid for herself and the twins and the children sat down. Clementine got the water bowl for Lavender and Mrs Mogg gave the little pig an extra brownie. She said it had fallen on the ground earlier and she was saving it especially for her.

Aunt Violet and Mrs Bottomley walked into the tent.

'Hello Aunt Violet. How are your tours going?' Clementine asked.

'Perfectly well, apart from that little monster Joshua Tribble. I found him in my bedroom teasing Pharaoh,' her great-aunt replied. 'But Mrs Bottomley dealt with him. I don't think he'll be trespassing anywhere ever again.'

Mrs Bottomley smiled, revealing a row of yellowed teeth. Clementine wondered what she'd done to him. She didn't like to think. Maybe she'd find Joshua in a cupboard later.

'Who's that?' Tilda whispered as the two women sat down at a nearby table.

'That's Mrs Bottomley. She was my teacher and now she's friends with Aunt Violet,' Clementine whispered back. 'I hope she's not our teacher this year.'

'I heard that, Clementine,' Mrs Bottomley snapped. 'And you'll be pleased to know that I have no intention of taking that class of yours ever again.'

Clementine's eyes widened. 'Yes!' she mouthed.

'Heard that too!' the woman barked.

The children giggled. They finished their treats and decided to take a wander around the stalls. Teddy suggested they go straight to the jumping castle but Araminta, sensible as always, said that they should probably let their afternoon tea go down for a while. She remembered when her brother and sister had ridden a merry-go-round at a fair right after lunch. The results hadn't been pretty.

Teddy and Tilda remembered too and decided to take their big sister's advice.

As well as Mrs Tribble's bric-a-brac and Father Bob's flowers, there was a man selling homemade cheese (which Clementine decided smelt like old socks), another lady had handcrafted baby clothes, and there was a pointy-looking fellow selling paintings. Mr Mogg had a wonderful vegetable stall with home-grown produce, too.

Clementine and her friends were hoping that there was something they could spend their pocket money on. 'What about the lucky dip?' Clementine suggested.

Over in Mrs Mogg's tent, Mrs Bottomley and Aunt Violet finished their tea and decided to take a walk too.

'What a lot of old tat,' Aunt Violet sneered at the cracked plates and chipped vases on Mrs Tribble's stall.

Ethel Bottomley had been admiring a very pretty teapot with a small chip on the rim but put it back down when she heard Aunt Violet's comment. She wandered further along and came to a lovely timber box.

'Oh, this is sweet. I could use that in the classroom for something.' She picked it up and examined the silky timber. 'How much is this one?'

Mrs Tribble looked at the box. She'd sold another smaller one earlier but couldn't remember the price.

'If you give me a moment I'll check.' She ran her finger down the list she'd been keeping of the sales.

Aunt Violet walked up beside Mrs Bottomley. She shook her head. 'Goodness, Ethel, what do you want that old rubbish for?'

'I thought it could come in handy for something. It's pretty, or at least it was once. There are always little bits and pieces – you know, blocks and the like – that I need containers for at school.'

Aunt Violet looked at the box more closely. Suddenly her memory flashed. She gasped.

'No, Ethel, you can't have it,' Aunt Violet said, reaching out to snatch it from her.

Mrs Bottomley clutched the box to her

ample chest. 'What are you doing, Violet? I want it and I'll have it.'

'No! You can't. It's not right for you. It won't go with the classroom decor!' Aunt Violet grabbed at the box.

By now the two women were attracting quite a bit of attention. Clementine looked up from where she was standing further along the row of trestle tables.

'What's Aunt Violet doing?' she asked, wrinkling her nose. 'Come on.' She motioned for her friends to follow.

Lady Clarissa walked out the front door and was horrified to see her aunt and Mrs Bottomley having an almighty tug of war. She raced over and stood in front of them.

'What are you two doing?'

'She can't have this,' gasped Aunt Violet. She was pulling as hard as she could. Mrs Bottomley was gripping the item with all her might.

'It's just an old music box from the attic, Aunt Violet. It's broken. If Mrs Bottomley wants it then she should have it,' Lady Clarissa called. She couldn't believe her eyes and neither could anyone else.

'It's not just an old box. It's my box,' Aunt Violet snapped. 'You should have asked me if you could sell it.'

Clementine, Tilda, Teddy and Araminta were standing beside Lady Clarissa, watching the two old women wrestling.

Basil and Ana were there too. Basil raised his camera to his face but Ana put out her hand.

'No, Basil, you can't take a photograph. They'd never forgive you.' Ana tried to stifle the grin that was tickling her lips.

'Give it to me, Ethel!'

'NO! I'm having it!' Mrs Bottomley shouted.

Joshua Tribble had heard the ruckus and come to investigate too. He roared with laughter at the two old women fighting.

'It's mine!' Aunt Violet bellowed and gave one last heave. Mrs Bottomley let go of the box and Aunt Violet went flying backwards, tumbling over Joshua Tribble.

'Cool, I didn't know old ladies could do somersaults,' said the boy. He crashed to the ground just as the box went soaring into the air.

'Noooooo!' Aunt Violet landed with a thud on her bottom.

The box fell to the ground and the lid sprang open.

There was a collective gasp from the crowd.

'Flash!' Tilda raced forward and looked into the box. She lifted the tortoise out.

'Is he all right?' Clementine asked, trying to see if his shell was still in one piece.

The little tortoise poked his head out and looked at the crowd.

'Oh, Tilda, that's wonderful. But how on earth did he get in there?' Ana said with a frown.

'The moving boxes,' Basil said. 'He must have been in one of the boxes I brought over for the attic. Poor old Flash will be starving.'

Aunt Violet was lying on the ground moaning softly.

'Are you all right, Aunt Violet?' Clementine looked down at her great-aunt, who opened her eyes and sat upright.

'No, of course I'm not all right. Ridiculous nonsense,' she spluttered.

Uncle Digby held out his hand to help her up.

Lady Clarissa eyeballed the woman. 'Aunt Violet, you couldn't possibly have known that Tilda's tortoise was in that box. So why did you want it?'

Clementine knelt down on the grass and looked inside the box. She noticed a lump in the lining at the bottom. 'Mummy, there's something in here.'

'Aunt Violet?' Lady Clarissa asked sharply. 'Are you going to tell me what it is?'

'If my memory serves me correctly, Clarissa, I think you'll find the missing Appleby neck- lace,' Aunt Violet said with a sniff.

There was another gasp from the crowd.

'Why didn't you just say so, Violet?' Mrs Bottomley pursed her lips. 'I would have given it back to you.'

'Because I suspect *someone* would have liked to keep that a secret, wouldn't they?' said Uncle Digby.

Clementine pulled back the lining of the box.

'Mummy, look! It's Granny's necklace from the painting.' Clementine held up the dazzling jewellery. It glinted in the sunshine.

'Oh, it's lovely.' Lady Clarissa took the long strand of diamonds and pearls from the girl. 'It's even more beautiful in real life.'

'It's mine, Clarissa,' Aunt Violet whispered.

Lady Clarissa shook her head.

'Aunt Violet, this was my mother's and before that it was Granny Appleby's and now it belongs to me. I've made a decision about the necklace and the matching earrings and tiara,' Lady Clarissa said. The rest of the set had been found some months beforehand and now resided in the safe in the library.

'What are you going to do?' Aunt Violet demanded.

'These jewels are so beautiful they should be in a museum. I'm never going to wear them and I doubt Clementine will either. But if we sell them, we'll have more than enough money to rebuild the hall and perhaps there'll be some left over to make the repairs on the house,' Lady Clarissa said firmly.

'No! You can't!' Aunt Violet's lip trembled.

'Aunt Violet, please try to think of someone other than yourself. Besides, I thought a new bathroom might be of some interest.'

The old woman sighed.

'Are you sure, Clarissa?' Mrs Mogg asked. 'You don't have to do that.'

'I know I don't. But what would I rather? That we have a priceless collection of unwearable jewels or that Clementine and her friends get to have ballet lessons and you have your quilting group, Maraget, and Father Bob has the flower show.'

'Clarissa, you're a marvel, my dear,' Father Bob declared.

'Don't thank me. Thank Clementine. It was her idea to clean out the attic. We might never have found the necklace otherwise.'

Clementine smiled. 'Will I get to wear a red tutu?'

Mrs Mogg smiled down at her. 'I'll start right away.'

Clementine looked at Tilda and Teddy and Araminta. Flash was nibbling on a piece of lettuce someone had found on the vegetable stall.

The four children grinned at one another.

'It wasn't just an old box after all, was it Mummy?'

'No, Clemmie.' Her mother shook her head. 'It was a box full of treasure.'

CAST OF CHARACTERS

The Appleby household

Clementine Rose
Appleby
Five-year-old daughter
of Lady Clarissa

Lavender
Clemmie's teacup pig

Lady Clarissa
Appleby
Clementine's mother
and the owner of
Penberthy House

Digby Pertwhistle
Butler at Penberthy
House

Aunt Violet Appleby	Clementine's grandfather's sister
Pharaoh	Aunt Violet's beloved sphynx cat

Friends and village folk

Margaret Mogg	Owner of the Penberthy Floss village shop
Father Bob	Village minister
Pierre Rousseau	Owner of Pierre's Patisserie in Highton Mill
Mrs Ethel Bottomley	Teacher at Ellery Prep
Mrs Tribble	Villager and mother of Joshua
Joshua Tribble	Boy in Clementine's class at school
Basil Hobbs	Documentary filmmaker and new neighbour

Ana Hobbs	Former prima ballerina and new neighbour
Araminta Hobbs	Ten-year-old daughter of Basil and Ana
Teddy Hobbs	Five-year-old twin son of Basil and Ana
Tilda Hobbs	Five-year-old twin daughter of Basil and Ana
Flash	Tilda and Teddy's pet tortoise

ABOUT THE AUTHOR

Jacqueline Harvey taught for many years in girls' boarding schools. She is the author of the bestselling Alice-Miranda series and the Clementine Rose series, and was awarded Honour Book in the 2006 Australian CBC Awards for her picture book *The Sound of the Sea*. She now writes full-time and is working on more Alice-Miranda and Clementine Rose adventures.

www.jacquelineharvey.com.au

Look out for Clementine Rose's next adventure

CLEMENTINE ROSE

and the Famous Friend

1 October 2014

Puzzles, quizzes and yummy things to cook

THE CLEMENTINE ROSE

Busy Day Book

1 October 2014

Loved the book?

There's so much more stuff to check out online